Swiftly Now

Swiftly Now

Carolyn Stoloff

OHIO UNIVERSITY PRESS

ATHENS, OHIO

By the Same Author

STEPPING OUT   (Unicorn Press, 1971)
DYING TO SURVIVE   (Doubleday and Co., 1973)
IN THE RED MEADOW   (New Rivers Press, 1973)
LIGHTER-THAN-NIGHT VERSE   (Red Hill Press, 1977)

Printed in the United States of America
Copyright © 1982 by Carolyn Stoloff
All rights reserved
FIRST EDITION

Library of Congress Cataloging in Publication Data

Stoloff, Carolyn.
    Swiftly now.

    I. Title.
PS3569.T623S9   811'.54   81-11150
ISBN 0-8214-0646-9   AACR2
ISBN 0-8214-0647-7 pbk.

To Henry Sauerwein, director, and the governing board of the Helene Wurlitzer Foundation of New Mexico where these poems came to light.

ACKNOWLEDGEMENTS

Poems included in this collection first appeared in the following publications:

The Windflower Home Almanac—AFTER LABOR DAY
Blue Buildings—SWIFTLY NOW
Blue Hotel—LOOK TO THE HILLS
Chouteau Review—FEET ON EARTH
City Bender—A CLEAN LIFELINE
Invisible City—EVENING MEAL
The Nation—A PIECE OF LIGHT
Open Places—IT'S EVENING IN THE SOUTHWEST
The Painted Bride Quarterly—AS MINUTES CHANGE PLACE
Poetry Now—BEHIND THE HOUR, LEAVING TAOS, NOON
Porch—ALL NIGHT THE TOWN CHOKED ON WIND, IN AN
    ARENA OF LIGHT, LORCA'S SILENCE, SOUTHWEST NIGHT
    SONG, WHEN MUSTARDS STAND FIRM-FOOTED BUT SHAKEN
Prairie Schooner—TRUCK FARMER
Silverfish Review—VESPERS
The Smith—NO FISH ABOUT
West Branch—HOW I GET OVER
Yankee—COLD, THE CHILL

The following poems appeared originally in *The New Yorker*:TOPOLOGY,
WITHOUT MILITARY NECESSITY, FROM A TOWN TRAFFICKED BY CRICKETS

The author is grateful to Robert Peters, Sonya Dorman, Clarelie Davis, and
her father, Charles I. Stoloff, for their helpful comments on the manuscript.

CONTENTS

FROM A TOWN TRAFFICKED BY CRICKETS

dust whirls
higher than singing wires

up there, a hawk—
sharp knife to ripe air

crows drop to a lawn   raucous
under a hissing spray

at my desk   near a window
not to be held captive

not to be fed mirages
from the glass box, I look out

green fringes
flutter on stiff limbs

I wait for pencils to flower
for sleep to produce its figs

       last night a voice
       broke from the packed clay

       to steep my name
       in the stillness

I hear an ambulance cruise
magpies, mounting   descending

and my heart—
a guarded fist of moisture

leaf lights through the window
set me rocking   rocking

in the sink's strainer
under a warm shower, a seed bursts—

the green body uncurls
it did not want to be captive

WHEN MUSTARDS STAND FIRM-FOOTED BUT SHAKEN

wind moves in
slate grey thunderheads
from the mountain

along the shrub line, leaves
lash the air
above, full-plumed
elms and poplars
swivel round and round

book in my lap   suspended
on a lawn chair
in my seedy field
(my line on the life staff
between worm and wing)
in the midst of a high-pitched ring
cicadas   crickets   harmonizing,

I hear the wind's velocity
sigh and hiss
through the trees' choir
and look up

from the pictured pyramid—
Imhotep's requiem in stone—

to the sky—a flooding Nile
thick with cloud hippopotami—
to breaks
of blue   spills of yellow
and wonder:

will it rain?
if I stayed would I be taken
by that wind   if I go
will I be taken

LORCA'S SILENCE

Lorca cut his thumb on silence
I soak up his silence with my bread

•

his silence—wide as an estuary—
collects on my lips

like foam, on flanks
of exhausted horses

•

when night's hard forehead
presses against me,

I smoke Lorca's silence   through seams
in the house of his poem

NO FISH ABOUT

tonight nothing shapes up
but a drop

a water seed
in a sea of solitude

     •

suspended, it collects
events of today   yesterday

broadcasts them all at once

on waves

  • • • • • • • •

bright drop
specific   boundless

what to measure you by

but another

a tap   a dog's bark
and you'd be
thinner than a stain

     • • • •

just past mine
there's a house of music

from it a languorous cat—
dauphin of the dark—

comes to lap
when there are no fish about

only silence
a drop

so deep
I could cast a line

A PIECE OF LIGHT
for Maggie Wymond

an ant drags a fly—
big as a truck to him—
up my wall   repeatedly
because it falls and the haul
must begin again

                    she says *we walked two years*
                    my soles are tough now

wet moonstones glow
under her brow
little green hands clap in sunlight
near her bare toes

                    when it snows in the mountains
                    we make a platform of pine boughs
                    it's cosy under the tarp

... with heat two can generate
returned to the high place
I add in thought

                    she says *I think the chop chop*
                    of an ax sounds blunter
                    and more honest
                    than a motor

a car leaves its choking dust-wake
on my phlox

Indians laugh and clap when we pass
people are good to us she says
and smiles

    we carry nuts beans grains
    in our packs
    in summer we boil lily buds

why must an ant make its home
so high   in my beams   I wonder

why do my hands all day search
the thick kingdom for sprouts
from seeds I planted
until the china sky
discolors at the rim
and living mountains
go flat in shadow

    she says *on winter nights we watch*
    pitch flare like a torch

. . . and I
shell my particular nut
for a piece of light

BETWEEN ROCK AND DREAM

for Virginia Mullen

in the lively zone
with friendly cows and the scorpion
we trip on shards
from our beginning,

crouch to examine crumbs
from old pueblos   and fall

into folds
resembling the sacred mountain
as it thrusts up
toward sun's many hands—

they spread luminous ointment
over our wounds

WITHOUT MILITARY NECESSITY

coming across   crossing by heart
menacing I suppose   drawn
to penumbral zones
positions staked out by sleep
I advance to shine among casualties
to shine in the desert night
a lamp of flesh
when the halo has dropped
and a pale moth whirrs
soundlessly around me

advancing behind a skin shade
between cricket passages
wool tufts on metal thorns
rose wounds opened in fur
I crush crisp black tanks
that cross me on scuttling threads
as silence opens its jaws
by the millions

FEET ON EARTH

a chemical breath
drifts my way

the embalmer's up early
preparing his guest

still cool . . . . time
to tend seedlings

I lift a sprout from the flat
poke a hole   ease it in

green shoots in a row
six inches between

below, claims overlap
mice worms roots interlace

if continents meet
in the sea's valleys

who   on earth
can be homeless

TRUCK FARMER

a man bends
over his crisp rows
wind rubs him like a cake of soap
breaks up his bed   shifts his dog
limbs creak

trailing oil of sage   skin
torn from sacred ponds
dust from dead pueblos, gusts
stroke him wrong

he flips his hat back—
to the west, sun
battles booming thunderheads

opaque   charged
with old needs, he hungers
for continuity

no sons to tend   but rows—
corn he'll snap from the stalks
turnips to tug   saffron cones
locked in

a man can't lie back and ride wind
like the sea   but oh
he is rocked

VESPERS

briefly a bird's cross
mars the sun's lustrous rose

the meadowlark   ventriloquist
casts
his quick clarinet

I'd like to thrust my spine
like a spear in earth
let it leaf!

and glide like sound
into the horizon's wound
running gold

SOUTHWEST NIGHT SONG

at night, when I've drawn the curtains
the beyond moves in—
dark choral mass

turning between sheets
a widow moans

penitents with open wounds
stagger across the plains

a rabbit's white patch
zigzags   yells of hunters
galloping through the brush
trail out like *te deums*

I hear the pump and creak
as a man with a woman shrinks space

then the spirit comes
flattening alfalfa and beardtongues
walls make no difference

on odd days
an Indian wrapped in blue
passes   we nod

DESERT SPINES IN MY SHOES

noon
mounts my shoulders

its clear gaze
lacquers
snakeweed's yellow tongues,

ignites
a wiry star

two butterflies dip   flicker
white flames

borne off by my breath

underfoot, an empire's
pyramid

grains
in deep chambers

not an ant in sight

hills fade in whole light
like greatness   like Moses,
trails on the plain

a sorcerer flaps
his black cape

beak agape, he rides
the ineffable bright tide

HOW I GET OVER

for Russell Adams

I dance in place
can't put my foot on the small stone
to cross

over there   arms akimbo
you urge me on

it's useless

we bow deeply
howling with glee
at my inability

we're Japanese

you stamp
waggling your square head
stretch a stout stick to me

I grab hold   step
totter on the first rock

don't speak   no no
can't laugh now!

I'm poised
on the minute's tip

PASSAGE

walking through sun's
solid butter
I make a small shadow pool

stones
tap holes in my shoes

the feet of a rose bush
drink deep

••

hills slip
into noon's yellow skin,

a secret side rooted

in moist caves
lances ripen

where do valleys begin?

••

light is touch
casting an absence

who goes there?

no one
it's the light
I walk through

across days : pebbles
on the road—

barley size—

made monuments   toward dusk
by long

shadow-spills

            ..

and then
night's ocean

EVENING MEAL
before the shade is drawn
in the house that is all window

when sage exhales
its spiced scent in the cool

and the sky's a banquet of color

I step into the still balm
that soothes movement on anthills
even birds

and feet firm on the land
reach for radiant pheasant-clouds
and lambs from the fatted flock

wash them down
with a cool quart of sky

then turn to peach fluffs
above the eastern hills

I've eaten well

full-filled, I trudge home
heavy with the world,

vanishing   with me
into dark lips
closing the horizon

BEHIND THE HOUR

opening doors
loose on heaven's hinges
a blue stone rubbed on my eyes,

I watch swifts
practise departures
in the jittering sky

gusts come up strong
loosening green-gold clusters
of ripening plums

ragged locusts crawl
through the fine flour of sunlight—
old quirks   hard to shake

I lift a splintered skull—
four firm teeth

no strings attached
no sour grass scent
or mobile lip

sawdust from broken rock
spills
from its holes

dry bells rustle
I exchange breaths
with the dark nostrils

behind every hour

THE WIZARD WIND

tonight the wizard wind
plays with surfaces

your smile glows
through the mask on my mirror nail

once my bed was an open coffin
and you died in me,

exhausted by flight   arms
spilling over my shore

once you sought earth
and wrapped me around you

but this is another country
the mountains a distant rim

I watch light die behind them

anglo   how do you come
to dominate darkness,

walking the wind's high wire
turning the poplars white

go back to your constellation—
mind over water

if you break
from behind the mask

to fling your winged body against me

I'll kick you under the rug
return you to dust

shut my house to wind
nail the lid down

sealing the mask's lips
with mine

IT'S EVENING IN THE SOUTHWEST

even the aspen leaves hold still
in the still air gold as beer

a long way off, mountains crawl
along the bottom of the sky's sea

silence hovers like bees
in evening's mouth
as I unfold your letter and catch—

between proudhumble accounts
of your accomplishments—

something moving
mourning the rift   a Rio Grande gorge
between us

you could still slip
into it with me   easily

but you don't want ease
you want to stand at the edge

of the pit you carry
dropping daggers and skulls
from old wrecks and new campaigns,

listening for echoes
as though they'd sing

I heard you passed through town
I know you made no connection

you trust this new frequency
to paper only, I suppose—
it's safe that way

the surge comes through
a south wind between your words

I let it   because it's late
edges of clouds in the west flush
richly   suddenly,

now that the sun has sunk in the silt
and heart-shaped poplar leaves
lose color

even the lark is still
darkness absorbs the trees

I sway somewhat like seaweed
with them in the night water

to the east, meteor dust glows
like a man-of-war

ALL NIGHT THE TOWN CHOKED ON WIND

a dog barked at the moving darkness

like army ants,
dust advanced   searching for lizards
to bury

a mouse in my breadbox
heard the moon behind clouds
and scrambled to the beams

the lion came
from an angry distance
and a wolf from the outer skin
carrying seeds of dead stars
between his paw pads

what had I said
to deserve this itch in my covering
dry as a vacant pod,

to be harassed
by despair's absence

all night the wild breath
blew crisp weeds into ditches,

clogged wells where I drew my voice

all night
death's dice rattled
never settling

where night met day, an ember
flared
in the hooting hearth

IN AN ARENA OF LIGHT
the onion I peel glows
moon-in-hand

framed in the window, weeds
by Holbein
strain toward plume

a whistle . . . .
two bullets whizz
it's a hummingbird chase

one's back

his slim tongue collects tax
from the hollyhocks

my tongue   made an oaf
has me cooking something gross
from Istanbul—
roots   lamb

I wait for scum to boil up
for words   I wait
. . . a thick honey in my veins

vexed by contentment, I step out
to tug
noon's platinum tresses

they hold

as though no deaths had been swept
under the green rug,

only bright dust

NOON

sun throws a cashmere cloth
on what it sees of me
whichever way I turn

I open my armpits
sun leaps into them

when I bend to gather rose hips
nursing my own shadow
sun takes me from behind

can I be cool to it?

blood pearls tinkle in my palm
I nip one
grinding compressed centers

my tongue in its cave
of treasured moisture
stirs among them

Cyclops sky   grave earth
in my bush a rose opens

LOOK TO THE HILLS

for Jim Cervantes

once breath of the herd roared
down my corridors
rivers slid from the sky—

silk on my skin
on the roof, a drum roll

now cottonwood pods spill
before me in the dust   a raven
walks like a mourner,

awkward and serious   so I veer
into whiskered grains,
yellow blossoms like lint caught

a horse—nose deep—
smells the cool shadow
coming   and looks up

each day I walk to a hill
loaded with whispershells
evenings, I tear at the slope

tracking death
by its crumbs of sleep
to the dark loaf

WHEN YOU COME CALLING

for Maggie Wymond

we slice a loaf   watch heat
spire upward in the hearth
exchange basalt   moonstone,

news of your white donkey
and the strange light

your skirt   stained green
passed through wilderness

it smells of artemisia
and smoke
from fire kindled on parched clay

as you speak, I see faces
lit from below

now you—risen for water
in the dark—look up

I too
when the town current failed
. . . from my yard

flinging out rings, it shimmers
above the earth hump
where old powers sleep

at our elbows, the sceptic . . . .

night knocks

you slip into its dark
faery cape

AFTER LABOR DAY

I've watched grasshoppers proceed
this way or that   up
around   under pigweed

now a click   a leap
a gasp of vermilion skirts
gorgeous!
one's hovering
clacking her castanets
for minutes

at last
she plops to earth

olé gay lady
that was some
gypsy burst

one of these days
you'll sink
your ovipositor
in the clay

then   labor over
tatterdemalion, you'll crawl
under some dry rosette

I used to wonder where you go
I guess I know
a spring   a summer   and one fall
that's it

A CLEAN LIFELINE

when the sun
slips toward the hills—

those *carabineros*
caped in mauve—

I strap on my car   go
straight as a saw
on a road
frayed with clover

it's the space
between us
I adore

at the rim
sun's juice thickens
to a gold syrup

acres of sage . . . here,

no pope has raised
his umbrella

a hawk   adrift
in his house

sights me—

I'm swift as a mouse

SWIFTLY NOW

swifts eddy and loop
testing
the September tides

scattered armies
lay egg-mines
in the crackling fields

along the road, sunflowers'
rays have shrivelled
and let go

the mountains seem less blue

white spheres dehisce
and the threads blow

let go   let go

in the west, tufts flare
and fade
swiftly now

far off   down the long pasture
horses in silhouette
small as piano hammers   cluster
against chill gusts

then the heavens glow
in one great chord—
gold as the gold sunflowers
have given up

a bird drops
to a brown fist
asway on its hairy stem
to tug a seed from its cell

earth's dark

flower heads   darker still
litter the asphalt
notes   at rest

what won't give gracefully
breaks I guess

SALLYING FORTH

against the clear mountains
mother comes to hand
from her postmark
she sends seven silver fingers
father waves from Mt. Sinai

with a new year in my pocket
I rev up   reverse
re-enter my circuit
flow to the farmers' market
an engagement with green petticoats
finger-long radishes
fat as moles   and plump
red clappers still warm
just plucked from the cord

I meet crackling eyes
exchange breaths   estimates
of endurance
prospects seem good
coins slide into cracked palms

I bear my ballast home
still tingling, I unload
compose myself
and begin the sorting

AS MINUTES CHANGE PLACE

a tungsten butterfly
alights

      on a naked stalk

the hour glows
in its bulb

leaf shades   bruises
swarm over me

      clouds progress
      chromatic scales

I can't pluck the tunes—
just out of reach
under my dark coat

      I call for postponement

      to leave my palm print
      on plaster

a few motes catch sun
live again

yes, there!   lilacs
so thick you can't see the green

that girl who pins up her hair
I was she

galaxies   trapped
in a glass marble

      between thumb and forefinger
      ...gone...

rose hips countless as stars
ask to be picked

to fill jars
with seconds that wheel away
flung from a fist

     still I keep pace
     over the unrolling bolt

the swift
have been eaten by wind

     soon wind will topple
     my flowerpot

FEEDING TIME

pouring seeds
through the minute's waist
I feel the sack's belly go

like a cloud
returning white grains
to black oceans

THE SHAPE OF MOTION

a music with me for days

in spells, black birds
pepper veins between destinations

slowly flapping, I've tried
to follow them
back to a distant whistle

an apple for the burro
to recall tender beginnings

touched, they take the shape
of motion—

unkempt laughter
quivering the aspens

I set out on foot for the desert
its buttes robed in light

crystals
slide past my fingers   and glass
the disordered mineral

and all around   in my palm
beneath the surface   in wells—

dark birds
the sky   deep and cool

light glides down high walls
voices
from hushed rooms

here, the small cup of tears
a secret bush to hide in

singing through canyons
I may touch   in half-light

my back   disappearing
around a boulder

as though hurrying home

TOPOLOGY

I walk dark alleys
even between wild roses
powdered with road dust

evening—
one clear lark call

behind it I hear
a wood thrush
singing in distant hemlocks

here, space
takes my breath

to China
where liquid light
rises in the bowl

and to some eastern barn
where cows—pilloried

over a trough—
turn straw
with thick tongues

in Holland they stand
to the knees in golden water

Ethiopian hands
plait black grass into boat-shaped baskets

where I walk, the road
parts a field's stiff hairs

evening opens a door
in the mountains
letting darkness out

shadows stones cast
turn to swallow them

Lord, even at the bottom I know
valleys everywhere
climb

RELIQUARIES

in the yard, crooked combs
stand large
clotted with cloud-fur

the ground's white   drowsy

she sets the ash bag
beyond the door

a few embers
still lustful   burn
through the brown paper

inside   on the table
a boxed princess
smiling behind cellophane, waits
with closed eyes
for her fable

the woman tapes the giftwrap
at the ends   knots
loops the red ribbon

now the pinned specimen—
spread wings veined
like church windows—a saint,
wasps (if they were men)
would worship

at a gust
of laughter from outside
she looks through the pane

a snow clump, torn from its limb,
sugars the air briefly
like a bride

COLD

this morning glass fish
nibble the elm

solid transparent sadness
grips the twigs

there's a great scissors . . .
the crackle of dismemberment

next door a car gasps   gags

framed in a truck window
a chimpanzee in a crocheted shawl
grins in passing

what the lonely will settle for!

plundering birds
peck the day's suet flesh

at dusk, chained wheels on the road
. . . slapping wind

a justice of the peace opens his office
in the earth

never a last love I say
putting a match to the kindling

SARABAND FOR A DEPARTURE

I pack Tillie's preserves
boiled thick from the plums
I picked

I pack a tree   torn
from an elk's brow

three brown men
wrapped in blankets lean
on an earth wall
I pack them

and yellow apples
frozen to their limbs

like friends
in constellations

one bright ball
rolls a slow arc
through our cobalt hall

beyond the hills
I'll take its parallax again
when with the clouds

I'm borne
to the unburdening

THE CHILL

oh stern winter pool,
you show how a nail
driven in water
enters its opposite

how the wound closes
over a drowned gesture

LEAVING TAOS

a red moon
under glass
has been hoisted again
to the large nail

what I lived
and leave with
has been pressed into boxes

the cottage
is almost bare

I have seen
brick-colored mountains
turn purple—

a royal dying

and sparse viridian
seem to spread
like spring grass
across the mesa

but no red moon

Red   my horse
turned his head homeward
against my tug

and clouds—caught
by a low sun—

burned at the edges
like old love letters